Copyright © 1993 by Nord-Süd Verlag AG, Gossau Zürich, Switzerland
First published in Switzerland under the title *Der Sterngrauch Nimmersatt*
English translation copyright © 1993 by Naomi Lewis

First published in the United States, Great Britain, Canada,
Australia, and New Zealand in 1993 by North-South Books,
an imprint of Nord-Süd Verlag AG, Gossau Zürich, Switzerland.

Distributed in the United States by North-South Books Inc., New York.

Library of Congress Cataloging-in-Publication Data is available.
ISBN 1-55858-121-9 (trade binding)
ISBN 1-55858-196-0 (library binding)

British Library Cataloguing in Publication Data
Baumann, Kurt
Hungry One
I. Title  II. Lewis, Naomi
III. Eidrigevcius, Stasys
833.914
ISBN 1-55858-121-9

1 3 5 7 9 10 8 6 4 2
Printed in Belgium

*The color illustrations for this book consist of
photographs of models wearing masks made
by the artist. The masks were created with
pastels and tempera on cardboard. The
black-and-white illustrations
are pencil drawings.*

# THE HUNGRY ONE

A Poem by Kurt Baumann
Translated and Adapted by Naomi Lewis
Illustrated by Stasys Eidrigevičius

NORTH-SOUTH BOOKS · NEW YORK

STRANGE is the tale of Rum Tum Tum,
Who felt so empty and so glum
He'd eat a field and all things in it,
Then look for more in half a minute.
Feared by all and loved by none,
He was called the Hungry One.

The miller's precious garden thrived
Until the Hungry One arrived.
Lettuce, apple, onion, plum
Were gobbled up by Rum Tum Tum.
The miller raged: "What have you done?"
He only laughed, the Hungry One.

The miller's daughter made him stare.
He liked her hair, so long, so fair,
Her smile meant mischief—could it be?
*What has this maiden done to me?*
But first things first. He felt so thin,
Those turnips must go down within.

*I need more food—no time to talk.*
He ate the turnips, earth and stalk.
A hundred carrots promptly follow—
But even these don't fill the hollow.

What next? The trees; he'd had the fruits.
So ate the branches, trunks and roots,
And in the forest, dark and grim,
Devoured the trees that sheltered him.

Empty still, he sat and pined.
And then a notion cheered his mind:
*The miller's daughter I shall wed.*
"Girl, I ask your hand," he said.

Teasing again, the saucy miss
Held out her hand. He pondered this.
But then the miller roared, "What life
Would you have as a monster's wife?
My farm and mill would be a crumb
To that devouring Rum Tum Tum.
If I'd a wish, he'd disappear
And work disaster far from here.
I'd sooner have a man of straw
Than that thing for a son-in-law."

Rum Tum, unbeaten, answered plain,
"Now, now, good miller, think again.
I've lived too long without a wife.
She'd give me what I've lacked in life.
I grew without a mother's love—
No happy home, no roof above.
To seek the care I've never known,
I roam the world, alone, alone.
That's why my eating's never done.
That's why I'm called the Hungry One.
For guzzle, guzzle as I will,
I'm empty still, I'm empty still."
But all the miller said was, "No!
Tell your sad tale elsewhere—go!"

Well, go he did. Some peace at last—
Indeed, till seven years had passed.
And then one Sunday, who should come
From morning church but Rum Tum Tum!
How smart he looked! He hailed the two:
"Miller and Miss, good day to you.
I think a little debt is due.
I loved your daughter, begged her hand.
You scorned me, kicked me off your land.
Now I shall eat her; she'll be mine,
And then on you yourself I'll dine.
Don't plead. Don't pray. 'Twill soon be done.
For I am still the Hungry One."

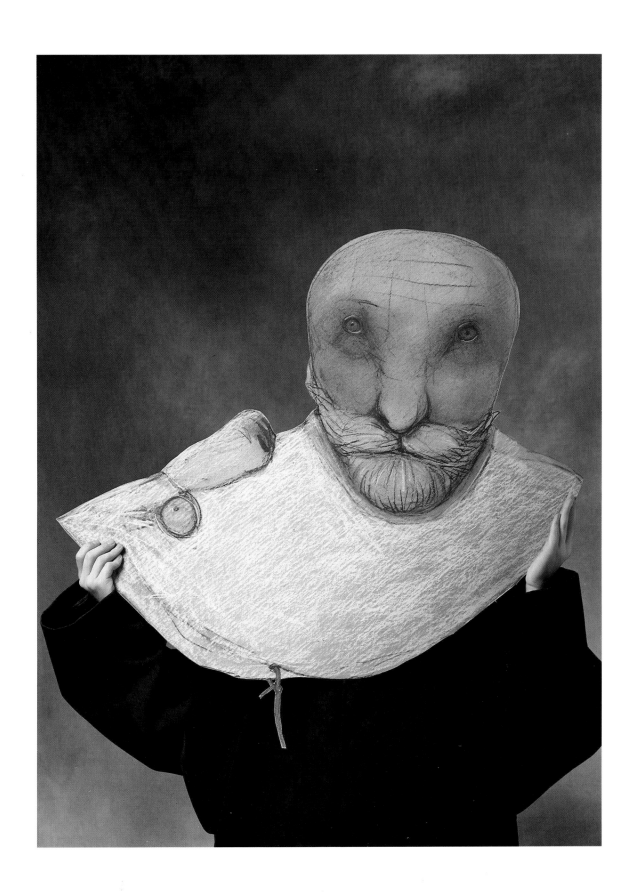

Straightaway the feast began.
He ate the maid, he ate the man.
He ate the mill from sail to rafter.
They jailed him and he shook with laughter.
Why did he laugh in prison cell?
Turn the page; the page will tell.

The heavy chains around him laced,
*Crunch!* He devoured them—liked the taste.

Three warders who disturbed his lunch
He dealt with next—an easy munch.
Then one by one, quite daintily,
He ate the bars and then, when free—

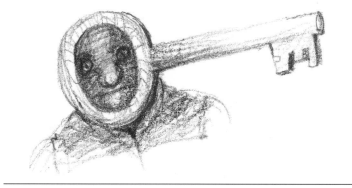

A leap! He was away, away.
He's vanished—where?—I cannot say.